THIS CANDLEWICK BOOK BELONGS TO:

The Animal Hedge

PAUL FLEISCHMAN
The Animal Hedge

illustrated by
BAGRAM IBATOULLINE

CANDLEWICK PRESS
CAMBRIDGE, MASSACHUSETTS

THERE ONCE LIVED A FARMER whose heart glowed like a hot wood stove with the love of animals. His greatest joy was to watch chicks become chickens. And piglets become pigs. And calves become cows.

The farmer lived with his three sons. All day long they toiled on the farm, singing while they worked.

His eldest son led them in coachmen's songs. His second son liked to sing songs of the sea. His youngest son's favorite was about a traveling fiddler.

But the farmer always chose
songs of the barnyard, of sheep
being shorn and colts being born and
ducklings trailing behind their mothers.

In the evening, he spoke to his animals
while feeding them. He rubbed their noses,
scratched their backs, and smiled
to see how they'd grown.

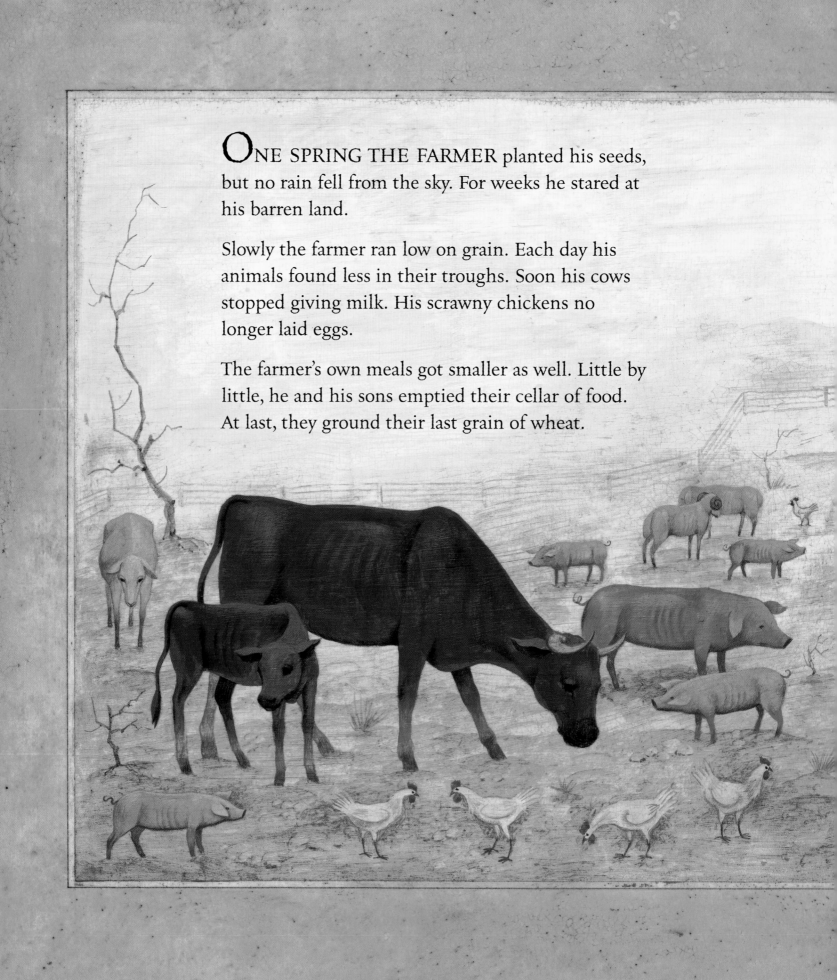

ONE SPRING THE FARMER planted his seeds, but no rain fell from the sky. For weeks he stared at his barren land.

Slowly the farmer ran low on grain. Each day his animals found less in their troughs. Soon his cows stopped giving milk. His scrawny chickens no longer laid eggs.

The farmer's own meals got smaller as well. Little by little, he and his sons emptied their cellar of food. At last, they ground their last grain of wheat.

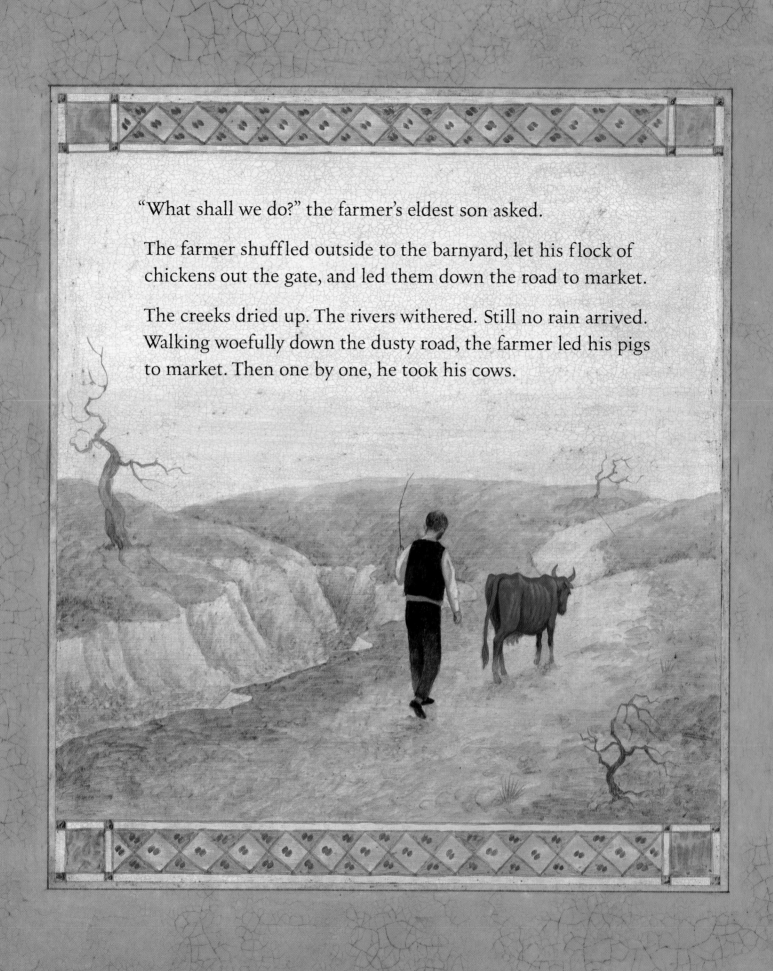

"What shall we do?" the farmer's eldest son asked.

The farmer shuffled outside to the barnyard, let his flock of chickens out the gate, and led them down the road to market.

The creeks dried up. The rivers withered. Still no rain arrived. Walking woefully down the dusty road, the farmer led his pigs to market. Then one by one, he took his cows.

And finally, to keep from starving, he sold his farm and moved his family to a tiny cottage with a hedge around it.

AT LAST, RAIN POURED DOWN from the clouds.
The rivers swelled and flowers appeared, but the farmer
was filled with gloom. For he no longer had his animals.
And he had no money to buy any more.

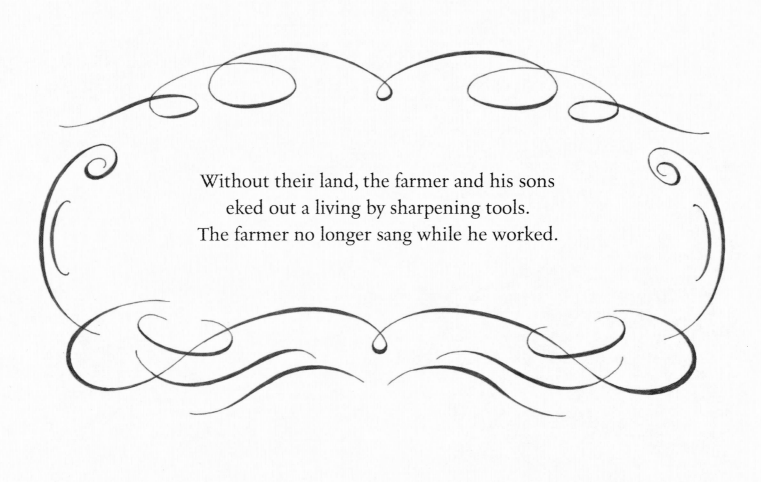

Without their land, the farmer and his sons
eked out a living by sharpening tools.
The farmer no longer sang while he worked.

Once again the farmer sang while he worked. In the evenings, he tended happily to the hedge. He trimmed the pigs' tails. He clipped the cows' horns. Softly, he spoke to the animals. To care for the hedge became his greatest pleasure.

In spring he brought forth from the hedge newborn animals. Ducklings and goslings, chicks and piglets all appeared close to the ground. With patient hands, the farmer nurtured his young—clipping them carefully, minding their shapes, watching them grow day by day.

Through fall and winter, he raised them into adults. The pigs grew plump. The calves became cows. One by one they took the older animals' places, and in spring more young would appear at their feet.

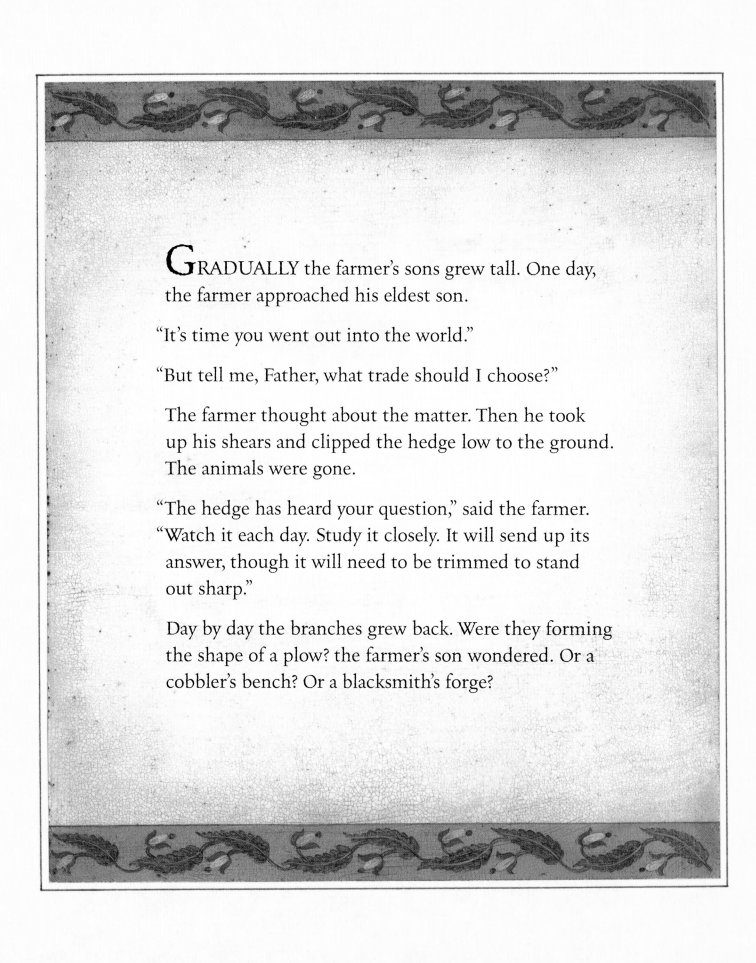

GRADUALLY the farmer's sons grew tall. One day, the farmer approached his eldest son.

"It's time you went out into the world."

"But tell me, Father, what trade should I choose?"

The farmer thought about the matter. Then he took up his shears and clipped the hedge low to the ground. The animals were gone.

"The hedge has heard your question," said the farmer. "Watch it each day. Study it closely. It will send up its answer, though it will need to be trimmed to stand out sharp."

Day by day the branches grew back. Were they forming the shape of a plow? the farmer's son wondered. Or a cobbler's bench? Or a blacksmith's forge?

For weeks he gazed at the hedge. Then one morning he glanced at it—and ran for the shears.

"But of course!" he shouted, staring at the branches. Swiftly, he trimmed the hedge.

And when he was through, he stood before a carriage hitched to a fine team of horses.

"A coachman, then, is it?" said the farmer to his son. "And how does that suit you?"

"Fine, Father, fine!" And he left home to take up his trade.

ONE DAY THE FARMER approached his second son.

"It's time you chose a calling for yourself."

"But, Father, what in the world should I be?"

Again the farmer clipped the hedge low, and for weeks his son watched as it grew. At last he recognized the shape of the branches and trimmed them into a great sailing ship.

"A sailor, then, is it?" said the farmer to his son. "And how does that suit you?"

"Fine, Father, fine!" And he set out on foot for the sea.

AFTER A WHILE THE FARMER approached his youngest son.

"It's time you went out into the world."

"But tell me, Father, what trade should I choose?"

Once more the farmer clipped the hedge, and day after day his son studied its shape. Then suddenly he saw the hedge's answer and trimmed it into a fiddler playing before a crowd of dancers.

"A fiddler, then, is it?" said the farmer to his son. "And how does that suit you?"

"Fine, Father, fine!" And he set out to take up his trade.

WITHOUT HIS SONS, the farmer was lonely. The house was silent but for his own footsteps. Longingly, he thought back to the mooing and quacking of his noisy barnyard.

Once again he clipped the hedge low and found chickens and goats and geese in its branches. Patiently he tended the animals as before, while one generation after another rose up.

ONE SUMMER the farmer's sons returned for a visit. The farmer was glad to find each of them happy in his trade.

"There's one thing that puzzles us," said the eldest son. "How did the hedge choose our callings so well?"

"It didn't," said the farmer.

His sons stared in surprise.

"The hedge never sent a coach up from the ground. Nor a sailing ship. Nor a fiddler. In truth, it's just a hedge like any other, and it sent up only branches."

The farmer's sons looked at one another in amazement. Slowly they realized that they'd seen in the hedge what lay deep in their hearts and heavy on their minds.

The three of them went out to look at the hedge. And there they saw what lay ever in their father's thoughts.

Excitedly, they pooled the money they'd saved. Together they walked down the road to the market.

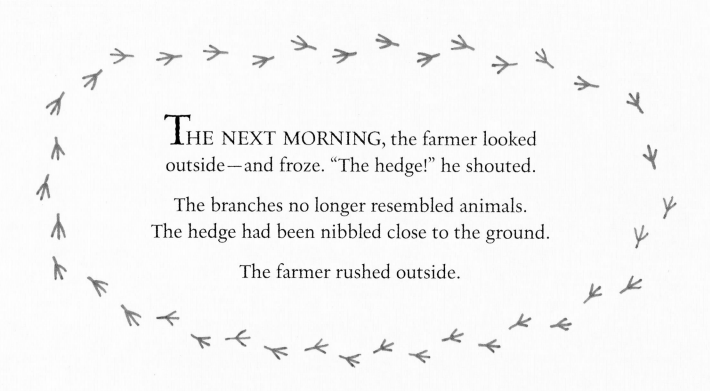

THE NEXT MORNING, the farmer looked
outside—and froze. "The hedge!" he shouted.

The branches no longer resembled animals.
The hedge had been nibbled close to the ground.

The farmer rushed outside.

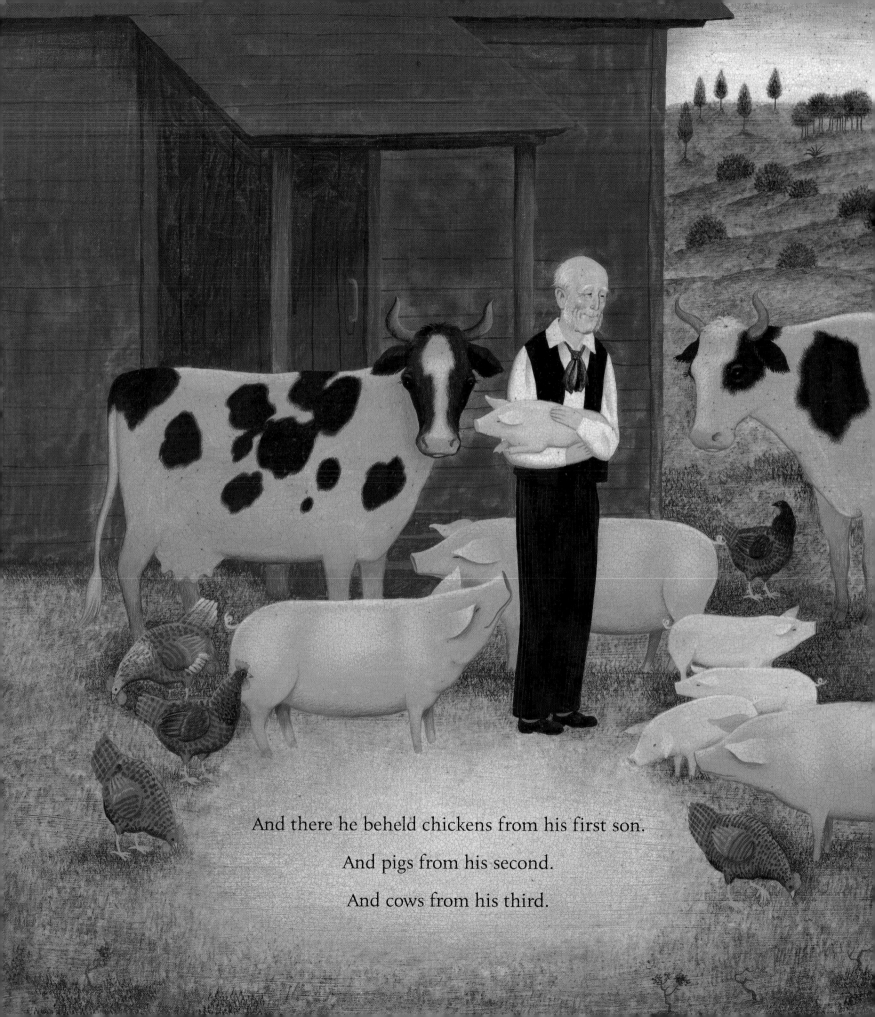

And there he beheld chickens from his first son.

And pigs from his second.

And cows from his third.

THE FARMER'S HEART
glowed like a hot wood stove.

And he made up his mind to let
the hedge grow back just as it pleased.

To Jane
P. F.

To Joe Stone
B. I.

Text copyright © 1983, 2003 by Paul Fleischman
Illustrations copyright © 2003 by Bagram Ibatoulline
Calligraphy by Judythe Sieck

First Candlewick Press paperback edition 2008

The Library of Congress has cataloged the hardcover edition as follows:

Fleischman, Paul.
The animal hedge / Paul Fleischman ;
illustrated by Bagram Ibatoulline. — 1st Candlewick Press ed.
p.   cm.
Summary: After being forced to sell the animals he loves, a farmer cuts
his hedge to look like them and teaches his sons about following their hearts.
ISBN 978-0-7636-1606-9 (hardcover)
[1. Farmers—Fiction. 2. Animals—Fiction. 3. Identity—Fiction. 4. Hedges—
Fiction. 5. Fathers and sons—Fiction.]   I. Ibatoulline, Bagram, ill. II. Title.
PZ7.F59918 An 2003
[E]—dc21   2002023751

ISBN 978-0-7636-3842-9 (paperback)

2 4 6 8 10 9 7 5 3 1

Printed in China

This book was typeset in Quercus Regular.
The illustrations were done in watercolor and gouache.

Candlewick Press
2067 Massachusetts Avenue
Cambridge, Massachusetts 02140

visit us at www.candlewick.com

Paul Fleischman is the award-winning author of many books for children and young adults, including *Joyful Noise: Poems for Two Voices,* winner of the Newbery Medal; *Graven Images,* a Newbery Honor Book; *Dateline: Troy,* an American Library Association Best Book for Young Adults; and *Weslandia,* an American Library Association Notable Children's Book. He lives in Aromas, California. "Growing up in Santa Monica, California," he recalls, "I used to walk past a hedge trimmed into animal shapes. I felt sure there was a story in that hedge — all I had to do was look for it, then trim it into shape."

Bagram Ibatoulline was born in Russia, graduated from the State Academic Institute of Arts in Moscow, and has worked in the fields of fine arts, graphic arts, mural design, and textile design. He illustrated *Crossing* by Philip Booth and *The Nightingale* by Hans Christian Andersen as retold by Stephen Mitchell. He is also the illustrator of *The Miraculous Journey of Edward Tulane* by Newbery Award winner Kate DiCamillo. He says, "As I was working on *The Animal Hedge,* I was most influenced by eighteenth- and nineteenth-century American folk art. I appreciate the naiveté of those untrained painters."